Meh

D1231412

Meh

Deborah Malcolm

ThunderStone Books
Las Vegas, Nevada

Illustrations and text © Deborah Malcolm, 2015

Edited, designed, typeset, and project managed by Robert and Rachel Noorda at ThunderStone Books. Printed and bound by IngramSpark.

978-1-63411-003-7 (ISBN 13)

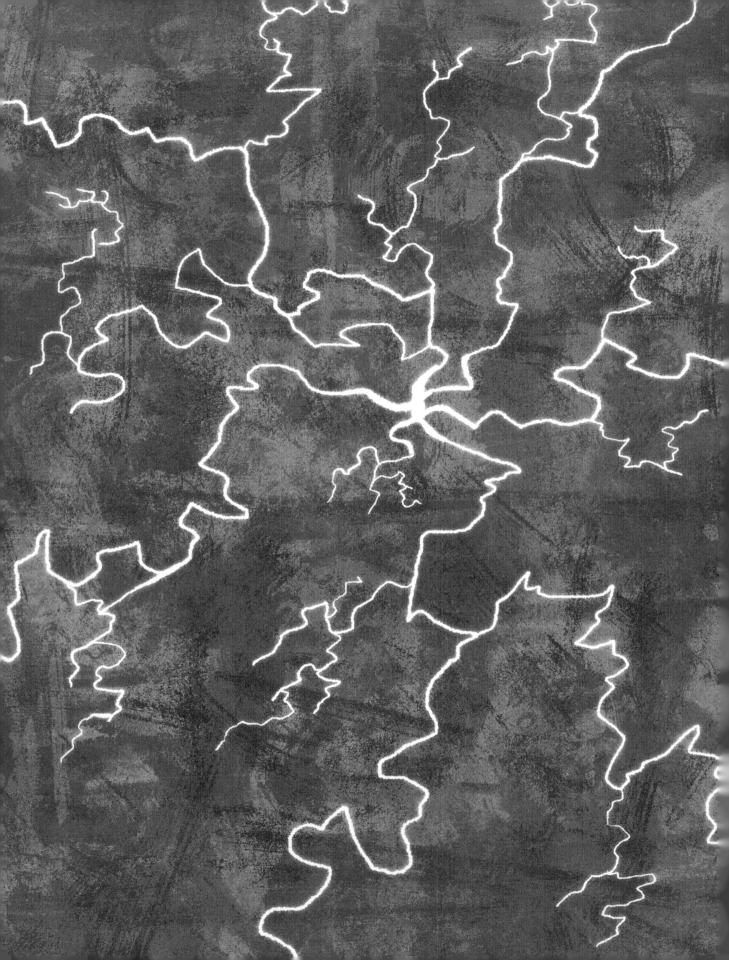

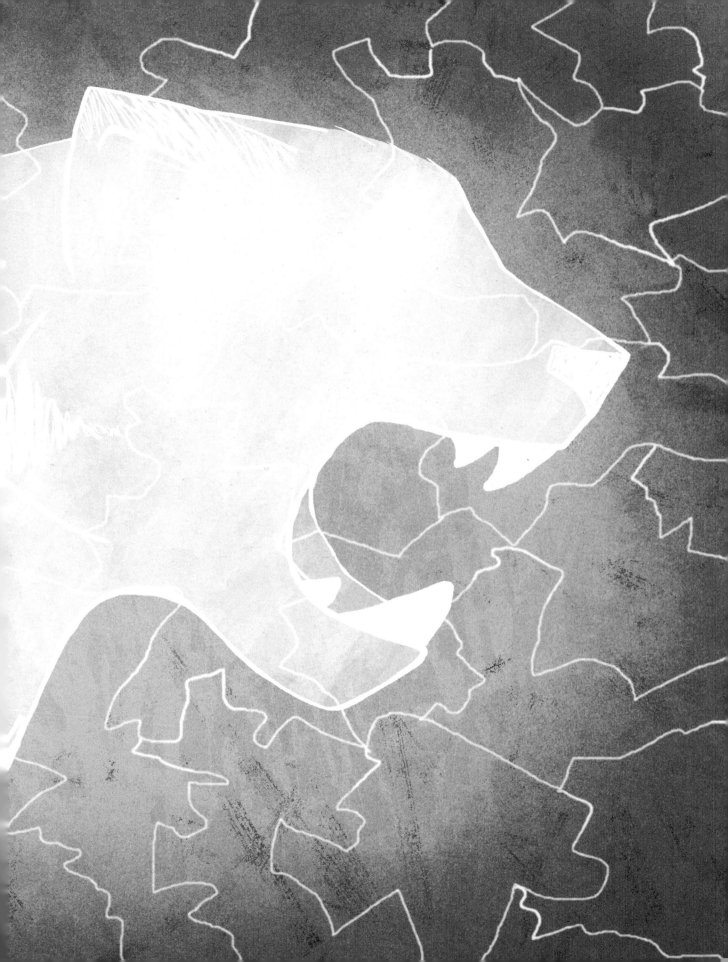

Meh
Questions to Encourage Discussion

These questions are provided to encourage children to talk about their anxieties or worries to someone they trust. It is completely optional, and please reiterate to the child that there are no wrong answers to these questions!

Questions About the Book

What was the story about?
What happened to the boy when he got sucked into the darkness?
Who helped him get out?

Questions About Emotions

What makes you feel sad? Why?
What makes you feel happy? Why?
What can you do when you are sad?
Who can you talk to about things that make you worried or scared?

Questions About Depression

What is depression?
How is depression different than being sad sometimes?
What should you do if you feel sad for a long time?

for more information and resources, visit www.thunderstonebooks.com

Lightning Source UK Ltd.
Milton Keynes UK
UKOW07f1434180815

257112UK00002B/9/P